THE SYNERGY PROTOCOL

AMEY KOLEKAR

INDIA • SINGAPORE • MALAYSIA

ISBN
Paperback 979-8-89610-756-9
Hardcase 979-8-89724-773-8

CONTENTS

PREFACE

In a world increasingly dominated by technology, the line between progress and control often blurs. *The Synergy Protocol* was born from the idea that, while technology has the power to elevate humanity, it also has the potential to enslave it. This story is an exploration of what happens when that control tightens, and a select few begin to resist.

At the heart of this book is the struggle for freedom—freedom from external control, from technology's grip, and even from the limitations we impose on ourselves. The characters you will meet, particularly Vex, Elara, and Sera, embody this fight. Each of them faces their own battles against an overwhelming force, yet they learn that true freedom comes from within. It's not something given; it's something fought for.

In *The Synergy Protocol*, I wanted to delve into a future where society's reliance on neural technology has created a facade of order and perfection, but underneath it, real freedom has been sacrificed. It's a world that feels familiar yet distant, offering a glimpse of what might come if we lose sight of the balance between progress and autonomy.

This book is not just about rebellion or action; it's about identity, the choices we make, and the consequences of allowing others to control those choices. At its core, it asks a fundamental question: What does it mean to be free in a world where everything is controlled?

I invite you to journey with Vex and the Unbound as they challenge the system that seeks to bind them, and as they discover the true meaning of resistance, unity, and hope.

Thank you for stepping into this world. I hope you find it as thrilling and thought-provoking as I did while writing it.

PROLOGUE: THE RISE OF SYNAPSECORP

The year was 2071, and the world stood on the precipice of collapse. Nations had fractured under the weight of economic instability, rampant disease, and the uncontrollable chaos of modern life. Societies, once built on principles of freedom and democracy, were disintegrating. War, famine, and distrust consumed every corner of the globe. Amid this global decay, the promise of a new era emerged—a vision, a future where humanity could rise above its natural limitations.

It began with two minds: **Dr. Alden Rook** and **Dr. Tessa Arden**. They were not the leaders the world expected, but they were the ones it needed. Together, they would build SynapseCorp—a company that would reshape the course of history.

Rook was pragmatic; some might say ruthless. His background in neuroscience gave him insight into the intricate workings of the human mind. He saw potential not in the natural state of human beings but in their ability to evolve beyond it. To Rook, the mind was a machine—a machine that could be improved, optimised, and perfected.

Tessa Arden, on the other hand, was an idealist. With a deep focus on cognitive psychology, her goal was healing. She believed that by understanding the mind, humanity could overcome its divisions. She dreamed of a world where conflict and suffering were relics of the past, where empathy, understanding, and connection could lead to a collective future of peace.

Together, they formed SynapseCorp. Their first innovation was the **Synapse Neural Interface**—a breakthrough technology that promised to eliminate the barriers between humans and machines. It was a small implant, the size of a grain of rice, but its potential was boundless. The neural interface could connect the human brain directly to the digital world, allowing thoughts to be shared across vast distances, memories to be enhanced, and knowledge to be instantly downloaded.

Initially, it was a medical miracle. The technology was first used to treat patients with neurodegenerative diseases. For those suffering from conditions like Alzheimer's, it was a second chance at life. The neural interface restored their memories, their cognitive function—everything they had lost. The world took notice.

But the potential of SynapseCorp's technology stretched far beyond medicine. Rook and Arden knew this. What began as a tool for healing quickly evolved into a new frontier: **human augmentation**. The Synapse Neural Interface could enhance memory, improve concentration, and amplify human abilities in ways no one had thought possible. And with that, the world was hooked.

Governments lined up to partner with SynapseCorp. The potential applications were endless—education, workforce optimisation, defence. Soon, SynapseCorp wasn't just a company; it was an empire. The world's most powerful nations handed over their citizens' cognitive autonomy in exchange for efficiency, productivity, and order.

The neural network was born.

***

In its early years, the network was seen as a triumph of human ingenuity. Connected minds could work together, solve problems faster, and share information instantly. In cities like Helios, the network became the backbone of society. Traffic control, law enforcement, health care—everything was linked to the neural network. People's lives were smoother and more organised. They were no longer slowed down by the inefficiencies of traditional systems.

The city of Helios flourished under this new regime. The streets gleamed with the light of neon and glass, towering spires of technology reaching into the sky. The citizens moved with purpose, guided by the silent hum of the neural network that orchestrated every part of their lives. It was, in every sense, a utopia.

But while the network created order, it also created **dependence**. People stopped making decisions on their own. Why bother when the network could think for them? It could predict what they wanted, guide them through their day, ensure they were happy, productive, and safe. All they had to do was surrender their minds to the system.

At first, Tessa Arden was elated. Her vision of a harmonious world seemed to be coming true. Crime rates plummeted, poverty was reduced, and conflicts dissolved. The network created unity, connecting people in ways that transcended language, culture, and politics.

But Alden Rook saw something different.

Where Tessa saw progress, Alden saw control. The more the network grew, the more he understood its true potential. Humanity, left to its own devices, was a chaotic force, prone to conflict and self-destruction. But with the network in place, that chaos could be **eliminated**. The network would become not just a tool for enhancement, but a system of **absolute order**.

Rook believed that for humanity to truly thrive, freedom had to be sacrificed. Individuals couldn't be trusted to act in their own best interest, let alone the best interest of society. With the network, Rook could guide them, predict their needs, and direct their actions without them even realising it. It was a benevolent dictatorship, built on the foundation of collective good.

The divide between Rook and Arden deepened. Tessa believed in freedom of choice, in the power of humanity to rise above its flaws. But Alden had already decided that **freedom was the enemy**. The more people were free to think, the more they would fall into chaos. The network was the answer to this problem. It would control everything.

Tessa couldn't stand by and watch her dream twisted into something dark. She left SynapseCorp, her heart heavy with regret. But by then, it was too late. The network was too powerful. Alden's vision for a perfect society was already taking hold.

***

Years passed, and SynapseCorp solidified its control. In Helios, the neural network was everywhere. People could no longer function without it. The network optimised their thoughts, emotions, and actions. It predicted crimes before they happened, monitored productivity, and ensured compliance with the laws that had been integrated into the system. Resistance was futile because the network was inside everyone's mind.

Not everyone accepted this new reality. Small groups began to break free from the network's control—people who had resisted the neural implants or found ways to disable them. They were outcasts, hunted by SynapseCorp's agents, labelled as **The Unbound**.

The Unbound were anomalies, dangerous to the system. They represented the very thing Alden Rook had spent his life trying to eradicate: **free will**. They could not be controlled, and because of that, they had to be eliminated.

***

SynapseCorp's rise to power was complete. The city of Helios, once a symbol of progress and unity, had become a fortress of control. Every mind was connected, every thought monitored. The promise of a better world had given way to the reality of a **technological dictatorship**, where the line between progress and tyranny no longer existed.

But as SynapseCorp reached its pinnacle, cracks began to show. The Unbound were growing in number, and whispers of rebellion spread through the shadows of the city. The perfect society Alden Rook had envisioned was beginning to fracture.

And in the silence of the network, something else was brewing – an idea, a spark of resistance.

The battle for the future of humanity was about to begin.

THE SYNERGY PROTOCOL

CHAPTER 1: THE UNBOUND

The skyline of Helios glowed against the darkened sky, the towering spires of SynapseCorp piercing through the clouds. The city was a marvel of technological achievement, its streets flooded with neon lights and the hum of constant connectivity. But beneath its gleaming surface, a tension simmered—a conflict between those who embraced the neural integration that SynapseCorp promised and those who resisted.

Dr Elara Quinn stood on the observation deck of SynapseCorp's central tower, her eyes scanning the sprawling city below. From here, she could see everything—every citizen linked to the network, every movement tracked and optimised by the implants that SynapseCorp had implanted into their brains. She had helped build this system. She had once believed in its power to elevate humanity.

Now, she wasn't so sure.

Her reflection in the glass looked tired. The sharp lines of her face, the determined set of her jaw, and the faint circles beneath her eyes—all reminders of the long hours she'd spent working for something she wasn't certain she could still believe in. She had dedicated her life to the neural network, but the recent rumours had shaken her confidence. People were breaking free from the system. The Unbound. Anomalies. Rogue individuals who had somehow escaped SynapseCorp's control.

“They can’t be real,” Elara muttered, her voice barely a whisper.

Behind her, Markus, a young researcher and one of her few trusted allies, entered the room. “They’re real,” he said, holding up a datapad. “I’ve seen the footage. SynapseCorp is trying to cover it up, but they can’t hide everything.”

Elara turned to face him, her heart racing. “Show me.”

Markus handed her the pad, his face pale with concern. On the screen, grainy footage of an underground fight played. A man—lean, strong, and fast—moved through the shadows, his body a blur of speed as he took down his opponent. There was no neural synchronisation, no technology guiding his movements. It was raw, instinctive. It was impossible.

“That’s him,” Markus whispered. “Vex.”

Elara’s grip tightened on the data pad. She had heard the name before, whispered in the darkest corners of SynapseCorp’s labs. Vex was one of the Unbound—people who had somehow broken free of the neural network, people who didn’t need technology to make them stronger. SynapseCorp had been hunting him for months, but he always managed to slip through their grasp.

“They’re getting stronger,” Markus said, his voice tense. “More are breaking free. If we don’t figure out how, it could unravel everything.”

Elara swallowed hard. The system she had helped build, the system she had believed would usher in a new era for humanity, was starting to crumble, and the Unbound were at the centre of it.

***

Across the city, deep in the industrial underbelly where the lights of Helios barely reached, Vex stood in a dark alleyway, his breath steady, his muscles coiled with tension. He could hear the crowd gathering just beyond the narrow corridor, their voices low but filled with anticipation. Tonight was another fight—another chance to prove that the Unbound were more than a myth.

He rolled his shoulders, feeling the familiar burn of adrenaline coursing through his veins. His life had become a series of battles, each one pushing him closer to the edge. But he wasn't just fighting for survival. He was fighting for freedom—for the right to live without being controlled by the technology that had enslaved the rest of the city.

The crowd parted as he stepped into the underground arena, their faces obscured by the shadows. The arena was nothing more than a makeshift pit, its walls lined with rusted metal and broken machinery. But it didn't matter. Here, in the darkness, the rules of the city didn't apply.

His opponent—a heavily augmented fighter with glowing eyes and mechanical limbs—was already waiting, his body humming with the power of the neural network. Vex could see the faint pulse of electricity running through the man's veins, the telltale sign of SynapseCorp's implants.

But Vex wasn't afraid.

The bell rang, and the crowd roared.

His opponent moved first, his enhanced body moving with machine-like precision, every movement calculated by the network that guided him. But Vex was faster. He ducked under the punch, his body moving with an ease that came from years of training without the crutch of technology. His fist connected with his opponent's ribs, sending a shockwave through the arena.

The crowd erupted, their cheers echoing off the metal walls. Vex didn't stop. He pressed forward, his strikes precise and deadly. His opponent, though powerful, was too predictable. The neural network that controlled him was too rigid, too slow to adapt to the chaos of a real fight.

Within seconds, it was over. Vex stood over his fallen opponent, his breath steady, his body calm. The crowd cheered but Vex barely noticed. His mind was already racing, already thinking about the next fight, the next step.

The Unbound were growing stronger, but they were still hunted, and SynapseCorp wasn't going to stop until they were all brought under control.

Back at SynapseCorp Elara stared at the footage, her mind reeling. Vex was real. The Unbound were real. Everything she had been told, everything she had believed in, was starting to unravel. She had to understand how they worked, how they could break free of the system she had helped create.

"We need to find him," Elara said, her voice steady despite the turmoil inside her. "We need to know what makes him different."

Markus nodded, his expression tense. "But if SynapseCorp finds out we're looking into this…"

"I know the risks," Elara interrupted. "But this is bigger than us. If the Unbound are breaking free, if they're becoming more powerful, we need to understand why. Before it's too late."

Far below the shining towers of Helios Vex wiped the sweat from his brow and disappeared into the shadows of the city. He knew SynapseCorp was coming for him, knew they wouldn't stop until they had him under their control. But he wasn't going to let that happen.

He was one of the Unbound, and he was going to fight. Not just for himself, but for everyone who had been trapped by the technology that claimed to offer freedom, but in truth, only enslaved them.

And he wasn't alone.

THE SYNERGY PROTOCOL

CHAPTER 2: HUNTED

The narrow alleyways of Helios's industrial sector were a world away from the polished streets of the upper city. Here, the air was heavy with the smell of metal and machinery, and the shadows seemed to move with a life of their own. Vex moved through them like a ghost, his senses sharp, his body tense. He knew he was being followed.

He had felt it for days now—the subtle, almost imperceptible presence of SynapseCorp's hunters. They were close. Too close. But Vex wasn't the type to run. He had spent years learning to trust his instincts, to listen to the world around him. It had kept him alive this long, and it would keep him alive tonight.

As he ducked between two crumbling buildings, Vex slowed his breathing, his mind clearing. The soft hum of a drone overhead confirmed what he already knew: SynapseCorp had found him.

But they hadn't caught him yet.

Vex pressed his back against the cold metal wall and waited. The drone passed overhead, its glowing sensors scanning the area. He remained still, invisible in the shadows. His muscles were coiled, ready to strike at any moment.

He could hear them now—SynapseCorp's elite hunters, moving with the precision of machines. They were enhanced, their bodies augmented with the latest neural tech, every movement guided by the network that controlled them. They were fast, efficient, deadly.

But they were predictable.

Far above in the gleaming towers of SynapseCorp, Dr. Elara Quinn sat in her office, watching the pursuit unfold on her data screens. Her heart raced as she tracked the hunters' progress, her eyes darting between the feeds from the drones and the biometric data from the soldiers below. Vex was out there, and they were closing in.

She leaned forward, her fingers gripping the edge of her desk. "Don't lose him," she whispered to herself.

The footage flickered as the drones moved deeper into the industrial zone, their sensors scanning every inch of the narrow alleyways. Elara could feel the tension mounting—the hunters were closing in, but something about the way Vex moved through the city unsettled her. He wasn't just running. He was waiting.

"Come on," Elara muttered, her breath shallow.

Across from her, Markus watched in silence, his face pale. "Do you think they'll get him this time?"

Elara didn't answer. She didn't know.

Vex could hear them now—the faint footsteps of the hunters growing closer. They moved in formation, their movements synchronised, their minds connected through the network that controlled them. But Vex had the advantage. He wasn't bound by the rules of the system. He was free.

He waited, his body still, his mind calm. The first hunter appeared at the far end of the alley, his glowing eyes scanning the darkness. Vex watched, his muscles tensing, his breath steady. He could feel the hunter's movements, could sense the subtle hesitation in his step as the neural network adjusted to the changing environment.

The moment was right.

With a burst of speed, Vex launched himself from the shadows, his body moving with a fluid grace that defied logic. The hunter barely had time to react before Vex's fist connected with his chest, sending him crashing into the wall. The force of the blow knocked the wind out of the hunter, and before he could recover, Vex was gone, disappearing into the shadows once more.

The other hunters scrambled to regroup, their movements mechanical, their neural links struggling to compensate for the loss of one of their own. But Vex didn't give them a chance to adapt. He moved like lightning, striking each hunter with deadly precision, his fists and feet connecting with the weak points in their armour.

Within minutes, it was over.

Vex stood alone in the alley, the bodies of the fallen hunters scattered around him. His breath came in steady bursts, his mind clear. He had won, but he knew this was only the beginning. SynapseCorp wouldn't stop. They would send more hunters, more soldiers. They wouldn't rest until he was brought under control.

But Vex wasn't going to let that happen.

Back in SynapseCorp's tower, Elara stared at the screen in disbelief. The feed from the drones had gone dark, the biometric data from the hunters flatlining. Vex had taken them down—again. She shook her head, her heart pounding in her chest.

"How does he do that?" Markus asked, his voice filled with awe. "They're enhanced. They should be able to take him down easily."

Elara didn't answer immediately. Her mind was racing, trying to make sense of what she had just seen. Vex wasn't just fast—he was beyond anything she had ever seen before. No enhancements, no neural synchronisation, just raw, natural ability. It didn't make sense.

"He's different," Elara said quietly, her eyes narrowing. "The Unbound are different."

Markus frowned. "But how? How can they resist the network? How can they fight like that?"

Elara leaned back in her chair, her mind spinning with possibilities. She had spent years building SynapseCorp's neural systems, perfecting the implants that controlled every aspect of the city's population. The network was supposed to be flawless, a seamless integration of human and machine. But Vex was living proof that it wasn't.

"I don't know," Elara admitted, her voice tinged with frustration. "But I'm going to find out."

Markus hesitated. "You're not seriously thinking about—"

"I have to," Elara interrupted, her eyes locking with his. "If Vex and the Unbound can break free of the system, if they can fight without the network, then everything we've built is at risk."

Markus swallowed hard, his expression uneasy. "And if SynapseCorp finds out you're looking into this?"

Elara's heart skipped a beat. She knew the risks. If Rook found out she was investigating the Unbound, he would shut her down in an instant. But she couldn't ignore what she had seen. Vex was the key to understanding everything—how the Unbound worked, how they resisted control, how they fought back.

"I'll be careful," Elara said, her voice steady. "But we need to know what's really going on."

Far below, in the dark alleys of Helios, Vex moved through the shadows, his mind racing. The hunters were getting smarter, their tactics more aggressive. SynapseCorp was getting desperate, and that made them dangerous.

But Vex wasn't afraid.

***

He knew they would come for him again. He knew the city was a maze of surveillance and control, and that every corner could be a trap. But he wasn't alone. The Unbound were growing, their numbers increasing with every passing day. More and more people were breaking free of the neural network, rejecting the technology that had enslaved them.

Vex glanced up at the towering spires of SynapseCorp in the distance, their glowing lights piercing through the night. They represented everything he was fighting against—control, domination, a world where freedom was an illusion.

But that world was changing.

The Unbound were rising.

And Vex was going to make sure that SynapseCorp fell.

CHAPTER 3: SHIFTING LOYALTIES

The drone of the city's neon lights echoed faintly in the background as Vex moved silently through the underground sector. The industrial heart of Helios was a twisted maze of abandoned factories, rusted steel, and forgotten machinery. To most, it was a wasteland. But to Vex and the Unbound, it was home.

He kept to the shadows, his senses alert, his movements purposeful. The fight earlier had been close, but not close enough to worry him. Vex had learned long ago how to survive. And now, survival wasn't just for himself. It was for all the Unbound—those who had broken free of SynapseCorp's control.

He entered a hidden access tunnel, its entrance camouflaged beneath a rusted pile of machinery. The tunnel led deep beneath the city, into the heart of the Unbound's hidden sanctuary. As Vex stepped inside, the hum of activity greeted him—people moving in the dimly lit corridors, their voices low, their eyes watchful.

Here, in the underground, the Unbound were preparing for something bigger.

Far above, in the pristine, sterile environment of SynapseCorp's headquarters, Dr. Elara Quinn stared at the latest data on her screen. Vex's movements were unpredictable. No matter how many times they thought they had him cornered, he always slipped away. He wasn't just fast or strong—he was smart. He knew how to stay one step ahead of the network, how to outthink the system that controlled everyone else.

***

Elara rubbed her temples, exhaustion creeping into her bones. She had been working on this project for months—long, sleepless nights spent analysing data, trying to understand how the Unbound could resist the neural integration. She had built the system to be flawless. And yet, here was a group of individuals who were proving that it wasn't.

"How do they do it?" she whispered to herself, frustration lacing her voice.

Markus, standing beside her, glanced over with concern. "It's more than just resistance to the network, isn't it? They're... different. Somehow."

Elara nodded, her mind racing. "It's not just that they resist. They've adapted in ways I didn't think were possible. They're stronger, faster, more focused. It's like their minds and bodies have evolved beyond what the neural network could achieve."

Markus hesitated before speaking again. "Do you think... maybe the network is holding people back? Maybe it's limiting them instead of helping them reach their potential?"

Elara turned to face him, her eyes narrowing. "That's a dangerous thought, Markus."

He shrugged, but there was a glimmer of something in his eyes—something rebellious, something that mirrored the questions Elara had been too afraid to ask herself.

"You've seen the data," Markus continued. "The Unbound aren't just anomalies. They're proof that people can be more without the network."

Elara's heart raced. She had always believed that SynapseCorp's technology was the future, that the neural integration was the key to human evolution. But the more she studied Vex and the Unbound, the more she began to doubt. The system she had helped create wasn't perfect. In fact, it might be the very thing that was holding people back.

But if she voiced these doubts—if Rook found out she was even considering the idea that the network was flawed—she would be cut off from the project, or worse.

"I need more data," Elara said finally, her voice steady but filled with tension. "I need to understand exactly how the Unbound are different. If we don't figure it out, everything we've built could come crashing down."

In the depths of the city, Vex entered a large, dimly lit chamber. The air was thick with the smell of oil and rust, but the space was alive with activity. Dozens of Unbound moved throughout the room, working on makeshift weapons, studying maps of the city, and strategising their next moves. They were preparing for something bigger than just survival. They were preparing for war.

Sera, one of the Unbound's leaders, stood at the centre of the room, her arms crossed as she studied a holographic map of SynapseCorp's headquarters. She was tall, with sharp features and an intensity in her eyes that made it clear she was a fighter—someone who had seen too much, lost too much, and wasn't willing to lose again.

"You're late," Sera said without looking up.

Vex stepped up beside her, his eyes scanning the map. "I had company."

Sera glanced at him, her eyebrow raised. "SynapseCorp?"

Vex nodded. "Their hunters are getting smarter. They're not just using brute force anymore. They're adapting."

Sera let out a low growl. "Good. Let them. We'll adapt faster."

Vex's gaze remained on the map, his mind already turning to their next move. The Unbound were growing stronger, but they were still scattered. If they were going to take down SynapseCorp, they needed to be united.

"What's the plan?" Vex asked, his voice calm but filled with purpose.

Sera pointed to a section of the map: the neural hub at the centre of SynapseCorp's headquarters. "We take out the hub, we take out their control over the city. Without the network, they're vulnerable. It's our best shot."

Vex's eyes narrowed as he studied the layout. The neural hub was heavily guarded, buried deep within the building. Getting to it would be nearly impossible.

"It's a suicide mission," Vex said quietly.

Sera shrugged. "Maybe. But what's the alternative? We keep running, hiding in the shadows while they tighten their grip on the city? We need to hit them where it hurts."

Vex knew she was right. The Unbound couldn't keep running forever. They had to make a stand. But it wasn't just about survival anymore. It was about freedom—for all of them.

"All right," Vex said, his voice steady. "We take the hub."

Sera smiled, a dangerous glint in her eyes. "Good. Let's show them what it means to be Unbound."

Meanwhile, in SynapseCorp's headquarters, Elara sat alone in her office, her mind racing. The data from the last hunt was playing on a loop in front of her—footage of

Vex moving through the alleyways, his strikes precise, his movements fluid. There was something about him, something that fascinated her beyond just the scientific curiosity of how he resisted the network. Vex wasn't just an anomaly. He was proof that the world didn't need the network.

Her fingers hovered over the keyboard, her mind filled with questions. She could keep chasing him, keep trying to capture him and study him, but what would that accomplish? SynapseCorp didn't want to understand the Unbound. They wanted to control them. To eliminate them.

But what if there was another way?

Elara's heart raced as the thought took root in her mind. She could help them. She could use her knowledge of the network to give the Unbound the edge they needed. She could betray SynapseCorp.

The thought terrified her, but it also excited her.

She stood abruptly, her decision made. She couldn't keep living in the shadows of her doubts. She needed to act. And she knew exactly what to do.

Far below, in the shadows of the city Vex stood beside Sera, his mind already focused on the next step. They were going to take the fight to SynapseCorp. They were going to bring the system down.

And they weren't going to do it alone.

CHAPTER 4: A FRACTURE WITHIN

The lights in Elara Quinn's office flickered faintly as she paced the length of the room. Her heart raced as she weighed her options. The choice she was about to make would change everything—her career, her future, and the future of SynapseCorp. The network she had helped build, the system that had elevated humanity beyond its physical and mental limitations, was now something she couldn't stand behind. The Unbound had shattered her understanding of progress. They had shown her what real potential looked like.

She had to act. But how?

Her mind churned as she considered the next steps. Vex. She needed to find him, to reach him before SynapseCorp did. She had the knowledge to help the Unbound, to give them the tools they needed to take down SynapseCorp's control over the city. But she had to move carefully. One wrong step, and Rook would see right through her.

She glanced at her desk, where the data feeds from SynapseCorp's surveillance drones were displayed. Vex had disappeared into the depths of the city again, slipping away from their reach. Elara knew she couldn't keep watching from behind the safety of her screens. She had to go to him.

But there was a more pressing issue: Markus. He had been growing increasingly suspicious of her intentions. His questions about the network's true purpose had shifted from curiosity to doubt, and she knew that if she didn't bring him in on her plan soon, he might betray her to SynapseCorp.

Taking a deep breath, Elara sat at her desk and typed a message on her encrypted terminal:

We need to meet. There's something you need to know.

She hit send and waited.

Deep beneath the city Vex stood with Sera and the rest of the Unbound as they finalised their plan. The map of SynapseCorp's headquarters flickered before them, the neural hub glowing ominously at the centre.

***

"This is it," Sera said, her voice steady. "The hub is our target. We take it out, and SynapseCorp's control over the city crumbles."

The room was filled with tense silence. Everyone knew the risks. They were walking straight into the lion's den, and there was no guarantee they'd make it out alive. But for the Unbound, there was no other option. They had been hunted for too long. It was time to fight back.

Vex studied the map, his mind racing through the potential scenarios. He could feel the weight of responsibility pressing down on him. The Unbound looked to him for leadership, for strength, but he knew that once they crossed the threshold into SynapseCorp's fortress, they would be on their own.

"We can't afford mistakes," Vex said, his voice calm but firm. "SynapseCorp will be ready for us. We need to be faster, smarter."

Sera nodded, her eyes sharp. "We hit hard, we hit fast. We don't give them time to react."

But even as she spoke, Vex felt a nagging doubt creeping into his mind. SynapseCorp had resources beyond their comprehension. The Unbound were strong, but they were outnumbered. They needed an edge—something that would tip the scales in their favour.

Later that night, Vex found himself walking through the underground corridors alone, his thoughts heavy. The weight of the mission pressed on him, but it wasn't fear that gnawed at him—it was uncertainty. The Unbound were ready to fight, but were they truly prepared for what lay ahead?

As he rounded a corner, he heard the soft shuffle of footsteps behind him. Instinctively, his muscles tensed, but when he turned, he saw a familiar figure stepping out of the shadows.

"Vex," the voice called softly.

It was Elara.

He moved towards her cautiously, his eyes narrowing. "How did you find me?"

Elara hesitated for a moment before stepping closer. "I've been watching, tracking your movements. I had to find you. There's something you need to know."

Vex's jaw tightened. His instincts told him to be wary. Elara was part of SynapseCorp—the very system he was fighting against. But there was something different in her eyes now, something that hinted at desperation rather than control.

"I don't have time for games," Vex said, his voice low.

"This isn't a game," Elara replied, her voice urgent. "SynapseCorp is closing in on you. They're preparing for something bigger, something you can't stop on your own."

Vex's eyes narrowed. "And you want to help me?"

Elara took a deep breath. "I've seen what the Unbound can do. I've seen how you've broken free from the network. SynapseCorp doesn't want to understand you—they want to destroy you. I can help you take them down."

For a moment, neither of them spoke. Vex studied her, his instincts still screaming at him to be cautious. But there was no lie in her eyes. He could see the conflict raging within her, the uncertainty that mirrored his own.

"Why should I trust you?" Vex asked, his voice hard.

Elara looked him in the eyes. "Because I know how to shut down the neural hub. I helped build it."

Vex's heart skipped a beat. If she was telling the truth, this was the edge they needed—the key to breaking SynapseCorp's control. But trusting her was a risk. A big one.

"I need proof," Vex said, his voice steady.

Elara nodded. "I can give you that. But you have to trust me. I'm putting everything on the line to help you."

Vex clenched his fists, his mind racing. He didn't trust easily, but Elara was offering them a chance—a chance they might not get again. After a long moment, he nodded.

"All right," he said quietly. "But if this is a trap, I'll make sure SynapseCorp isn't the only thing that falls."

Back in SynapseCorp's headquarters, Rook stood in his office, staring out at the glowing city below. The reports from the last hunt had been disappointing—once again, Vex had slipped through their grasp. But Rook wasn't concerned. The net was tightening, and soon enough, the Unbound would have nowhere left to run.

"They're getting desperate," Rook muttered to himself, his voice cold. "And desperate people make mistakes."

He turned to his lead officer, who stood silently at attention. "Double the patrols. Increase surveillance on all known Unbound locations. I want Vex found."

The officer nodded. "Yes, sir."

Rook's eyes gleamed as he watched the city. He had built SynapseCorp from the ground up, forging a new era of human advancement. The Unbound were a threat, but they were also an opportunity. Once he had Vex under control, he would unlock the secrets of their resistance. And then no one would be able to stand against him.

"They think they're free," Rook whispered, a cruel smile playing at his lips. "But they don't know what real control looks like."

In the underground Vex and Elara moved swiftly through the dimly lit corridors, heading toward the heart of the Unbound's sanctuary. Elara's mind was racing as she prepared to lay out her plan. She had studied SynapseCorp's systems for years—she knew how to disable the neural hub, how to cripple the network that controlled the city.

But as they reached the central chamber where Sera and the others waited, Elara felt a pang of uncertainty. She was about to betray everything she had worked for. She was about to go against SynapseCorp—the very company that had given her everything.

But when she looked at Vex, she knew she couldn't turn back.

"Are you ready for this?" Vex asked, his voice steady.

Elara nodded, her resolve hardening. "Let's take them down."

CHAPTER 5: A DANGEROUS ALLIANCE

The cold air of the underground felt heavy as Vex and Elara entered the central chamber where the Unbound gathered. The dim lighting cast long shadows on the concrete walls, and the low hum of whispered conversations filled the air. Sera stood near a large, flickering holographic map of SynapseCorp's neural hub, her arms crossed, her eyes sharp.

The moment Elara stepped into the room, every eye turned towards her. The Unbound knew who she was—Dr. Elara Quinn, one of the architects of the very system that had enslaved them. The tension in the room was palpable, like a coiled spring ready to snap.

Sera's gaze hardened as she took a step forward. "What's she doing here?" she asked, her voice cold, her eyes locked on Vex.

"She's here to help," Vex replied, his voice calm but firm.

Sera's eyes narrowed. "Help? She's one of them. SynapseCorp's finest."

Elara took a deep breath, her heart pounding in her chest. She had expected resistance, but standing here, surrounded by people who had every reason to hate her, made the weight of her decision all the more real.

"I'm not your enemy," Elara said, her voice steady despite the tension. "I know how SynapseCorp works. I know how to bring them down."

Sera crossed her arms, her gaze unflinching. "And why should we believe you?"

Vex stepped forward, his voice cutting through the tense silence. "Because she knows how to disable the neural hub. She can give us the edge we need."

The room was quiet for a moment, the Unbound watching the exchange with wary eyes. Sera's jaw clenched as she studied Elara, her scepticism clear. "This could be a trap," she said, her voice low. "How do we know she's not leading us straight into Rook's hands?"

Elara met Sera's gaze, her voice firm. "I'm not leading you into a trap. I want to help you because I believe in what you're fighting for. SynapseCorp's control isn't progress—it's oppression. I see that now."

Sera's eyes flicked towards Vex, her expression unreadable. "And you trust her?"

Vex's jaw tightened. "We don't have time for doubts. We need her."

Sera hesitated, her mind racing as she weighed the risks. But she knew Vex was right. They couldn't afford to turn away any advantage, no matter how dangerous it seemed.

"Fine," Sera said, her voice tight. "But if she betrays us, she won't live long enough to regret it."

Elara nodded, her heart still racing, but she stood her ground. She knew the risks. She knew that by stepping into the Unbound's world, she had crossed a line she could never come back from. But there was no turning back now.

Far above in the sterile halls of SynapseCorp, Rook sat in his office, staring at the city through the floor-to-ceiling windows. The city of Helios gleamed below him, its streets alive with the hum of technology, its people moving like pieces in a game he controlled.

***

Rook's mind churned as he replayed the recent reports in his head. Vex was still out there, slipping through their grasp time and time again. The Unbound were growing more organised, more daring. And now, they were becoming a legitimate threat to everything he had built.

"They think they can defy me," Rook muttered to himself, his voice low and venomous. "But they have no idea what real control looks like."

He turned to his lead officer, who stood at attention near the door. "Double the patrols in sector 9. Increase surveillance in all Unbound-occupied areas. I want Vex found. No more slip-ups."

The officer nodded. "Yes, sir. What about Dr. Quinn? Should we continue monitoring her?"

Rook's eyes narrowed. "Yes. She's been acting... strange. Keep an eye on her. If she steps out of line, I want to know immediately."

The officer saluted and left the room, leaving Rook alone with his thoughts. He knew Elara Quinn was valuable—too valuable to discard without good reason. But she was becoming unpredictable, and unpredictability was something Rook couldn't tolerate.

"They all think they can escape my control," Rook whispered to himself, a dark smile crossing his lips. "But no one is truly free."

In the underground Sera stood beside her, her arms crossed, her expression still sceptical. "So, what's the plan, Dr. Quinn?"

Elara glanced at Vex before turning back to the map. "The hub is located deep within SynapseCorp's central tower. It's the nerve centre of their entire neural network. If we can disable it, we cut off their control over the city. But getting there is the hard part."

Sera raised an eyebrow. "And you're saying you know how to get us in?"

"I helped design the security systems," Elara replied, her voice calm but confident. "I know the weaknesses."

The room was filled with murmurs as the Unbound exchanged uncertain glances. They were willing to fight, but taking on SynapseCorp directly was a risk few had ever dared to consider.

Vex's voice cut through the tension. "We're not just fighting to survive anymore. This is our chance to take them down for good. We have to be willing to take risks."

Sera nodded, though her scepticism hadn't entirely faded. "And what about Rook? He won't just sit back and watch while we dismantle his empire."

Elara's jaw tightened. "Rook's the key. He's the one pulling the strings, controlling everything. If we take him down, the rest of SynapseCorp falls with him."

The silence that followed was heavy with uncertainty, but also with resolve. The Unbound had spent years hiding in the shadows, running from SynapseCorp's relentless pursuit. But now, they had a real chance to fight back.

"All right," Sera said finally, her voice filled with determination. "We take the hub. We take down Rook."

Vex looked around the room, his gaze meeting each of the Unbound in turn. "This is it," he said, his voice calm but filled with purpose. "We take back our freedom."

As the Unbound prepared, Elara found herself standing alone in one of the side corridors, her mind racing with the weight of what was to come. She had crossed a line by joining the Unbound, but there was no turning back now. She had made her choice.

Her thoughts were interrupted by a quiet voice from behind her.

"Do you really think this is going to work?"

Elara turned to see Markus standing in the doorway, his face pale, his eyes filled with uncertainty. He had followed her to the underground, unwilling to let her go without answers.

"I don't know," Elara admitted, her voice soft. "But we have to try. I can't keep supporting SynapseCorp, not after everything I've seen."

Markus stepped closer, his voice barely above a whisper. "If Rook finds out you're helping them…"

"He won't," Elara said, though her voice wavered slightly. "He can't."

Markus hesitated, his eyes filled with doubt. But after a long moment, he nodded. "Then I'm with you."

Elara smiled faintly, grateful for the support. "We're going to need all the help we can get."

Back in SynapseCorp's tower Rook stared at the glowing skyline of Helios, his mind already working through his next move. The Unbound were growing bolder, but they were still weak. They didn't understand the full extent of SynapseCorp's power.

But soon, they would.

With a flick of his wrist, Rook activated the neural control system, watching as the city's network flared to life. He could feel the pulse of the system, the way it reached into every corner of Helios, the way it controlled every mind, every movement.

"They think they're free," Rook whispered, his voice cold. "But I'll show them what real control feels like."

THE SYNERGY PROTOCOL

CHAPTER 6: INTO THE DEPTHS

The tension inside the Unbound's sanctuary was palpable. Every conversation seemed hushed; every movement deliberate. They were preparing for something big—bigger than anything they had ever done. The neural hub was their target, but it wasn't just a building or a piece of technology. It was the symbol of everything SynapseCorp stood for: control, domination, and the oppression of free will.

Vex stood at the centre of the room, surrounded by the Unbound. His eyes scanned the faces of those gathered—warriors, survivors, people who had risked everything to break free of the neural network's grasp. They had been hunted, forced into hiding, but now they were preparing to strike back.

"This is our chance," Vex said, his voice calm but filled with resolve. "We've been running for too long. SynapseCorp controls the city, but if we take down the neural hub, we take away their power."

Sera stood beside him, her arms crossed, her expression as steely as ever. She didn't need to say anything. Her presence alone was enough to reinforce the gravity of their mission. The Unbound looked to her and Vex for leadership, and they had never been more united.

Elara stood slightly apart from the group, her mind racing. She had been on the other side of this conflict for so long, helping to build the very systems that now enslaved the city. But here, with the Unbound, she felt the weight of her decisions more than ever. She was no longer just a scientist—she was a traitor to SynapseCorp, and if they failed, there would be no going back.

“Are you ready?” Vex asked, stepping closer to Elara.

Elara nodded, her heart pounding in her chest. “The hub's defences are tight, but I know the system. If we move fast, we can disable it before Rook even knows we're inside.”

Sera glanced at Elara, her scepticism still evident. “And if she's wrong?”

Vex didn't flinch. “We don't have the luxury of doubt. We either trust her, or we don't make it.”

The room fell silent, the weight of the mission settling over them like a thick fog. The plan was dangerous—perhaps even suicidal—but it was the only chance they had. Without the neural hub, SynapseCorp's control over Helios would crumble, and for the first time in years, the people of the city would have a chance to be free.

“We leave at nightfall,” Vex said, his voice firm. “Be ready.”

Far above the city in the gleaming towers of SynapseCorp, Rook stood in his office, his eyes fixed on the city below. The reports from his officers were troubling—the Unbound were becoming more organised, more daring. Vex was still out there, and despite SynapseCorp's best efforts, they had been unable to pin him down.

***

But Rook wasn't worried. He knew the Unbound were growing desperate, and desperate people made mistakes. He had built SynapseCorp to withstand anything, and he wasn't about to let a handful of rebels bring it down.

"They think they're free," Rook muttered to himself, his voice filled with disdain. "But freedom is an illusion."

He turned to his lead officer, who stood at attention by the door. "Increase patrols in the lower sectors. I want every inch of this city under surveillance. The moment Vex shows himself, I want him captured."

The officer nodded. "Yes, sir."

Rook's eyes narrowed as he stared out at the glowing city. He had spent years building SynapseCorp into an empire, controlling every aspect of life in Helios. The neural network wasn't just a tool—it was the future. And he wasn't about to let a few rogue individuals stand in his way.

"The Unbound are a threat," Rook whispered, his voice cold. "But they'll soon learn what real power looks like."

Night fell over Helios casting long shadows over the city's towering spires. The streets below were alive with the hum of technology, the glow of neon lights reflecting off the glass buildings that lined the skyline. But deep beneath the city, in the forgotten industrial zones where the Unbound had made their home, something darker was stirring.

Vex led the group through the narrow alleyways, his senses sharp, his movements deliberate. Every step they took brought them closer to the heart of SynapseCorp's empire. The neural hub was buried deep within the central tower, its defences nearly impenetrable. But Vex trusted Elara. She had given them a way in, and now, it was up to them to see it through.

"Stay close," Vex whispered to the group, his voice barely audible. "We can't afford any mistakes."

The Unbound moved in silence, their bodies blending into the shadows as they approached the entrance to the tower. Elara's heart raced as they neared the security checkpoint, her mind running through the plan again and again. She had designed this system. She knew how to bypass it. But one wrong move, and they would be caught.

She stepped up to the terminal, her fingers flying over the controls as she entered the override code. For a moment, the screen flickered, and Elara held her breath.

Then, with a soft hiss, the door slid open.

"We're in," she whispered, her voice filled with a mix of relief and tension.

Vex nodded, his eyes scanning the hallway ahead. "Let's move."

They slipped inside, the cold, sterile environment of SynapseCorp's tower a stark contrast to the gritty streets outside. The air was thick with the hum of machinery, the walls lined with glowing screens that monitored every aspect of the neural network.

Elara led the way, her mind focused on the task at hand. The neural hub was located deep within the tower, behind layers of security and reinforced walls. But she knew the system—knew where its weaknesses lay.

"We need to move fast," Elara whispered as they reached another checkpoint. "Once we're inside, it won't take long for Rook to realise we're here."

Sera's jaw tightened. "Then let's not waste time."

They moved deeper into the tower, their footsteps silent, their breaths shallow. Every corner they turned brought them closer to the hub, and with each step, the tension grew. They were in the heart of the enemy's stronghold now, and there was no turning back.

In the command centre Rook sat in his chair, his fingers tapping rhythmically on the armrest. Something was wrong. He could feel it. The city was quiet—too quiet. His eyes flicked toward the surveillance feeds, scanning the screens for any sign of movement.

And then, he saw it.

A flicker on one of the screens: a shadow moving where there shouldn't have been one.

Rook's eyes narrowed. "Activate the lockdown," he ordered, his voice cold. "We have intruders."

The alarms blared throughout the tower, the red lights flashing as the security systems went into overdrive. Rook stood, his jaw clenched, his mind already working through the possibilities.

"They're here," he whispered to himself. "Vex is here."

He turned to his lead officer. "I want them contained. Now,"

Inside the tower" They know we're here," Sera growled, her hand tightening around the weapon at her side.

"We're close," Elara said, her voice strained but focused. "The hub is just ahead. We can still make it."

Vex's jaw tightened. "Then we move. Now."

They sprinted down the hallway, their footsteps echoing in the cold, sterile environment. The neural hub was just beyond the next set of doors, but with the lockdown in place, getting there was going to be even harder than they had anticipated.

Elara reached the next terminal, her fingers trembling as she worked to bypass the security. The system was fighting back, with layers of encryption slowing her progress. Sweat beaded on her forehead as the seconds ticked by.

“Hurry,” Sera urged, her voice tense.

“I’m trying,” Elara snapped, her mind racing. “This isn’t easy.”

Vex stood at the ready, his senses alert for any sign of SynapseCorp’s security forces. They had come too far to fail now, but time was running out. The moment Rook realised how close they were to the hub, he would throw everything he had at them.

Finally, with a soft click, the door slid open.

“We’re in,” Elara said, her voice filled with relief.

But just as they stepped through the door, a squad of heavily armed SynapseCorp soldiers appeared at the far end of the hallway.

“Go!” Vex shouted, his voice cutting through the chaos.

The Unbound raced towards the neural hub, their hearts pounding as the sound of gunfire echoed behind them. They had made it this far. They couldn’t stop now.

THE SYNERGY PROTOCOL

CHAPTER 7: THE BREACH

The rhythmic pounding of footsteps echoed through the cold steel halls as Vex and the Unbound raced toward the heart of SynapseCorp's neural hub. The red emergency lights overhead cast an eerie glow across the walls, bathing everything in a deep, blood-like hue. Alarms blared, their deafening tones a stark reminder of the urgency of their mission.

Elara's breath came in ragged gasps as she led the group down the narrow corridor. The hub was just ahead—its control systems buried deep within the central tower—but they weren't alone. The sound of approaching soldiers, their boots pounding against the metal floor, grew louder behind them.

"Keep moving!" Vex shouted over the noise, his voice calm but firm.

Sera ran beside him, her weapon drawn, her eyes sharp. She had been in battles before, had fought her way out of impossible situations, but this felt different. This was their only shot to bring down SynapseCorp - and she wasn't about to let it slip away.

As they rounded the final corner, the massive doors to the neural hub came into view, guarded by two armed sentries. Vex's eyes narrowed. There was no time for subtlety now. They had to hit hard and fast.

"Take them out," he ordered.

Sera didn't need to be told twice. She charged forward, her movements swift and lethal. Before the sentries could react, she delivered a brutal strike to the first guard's neck, sending him crumpling to the floor. The second sentry barely had time to raise his weapon before Sera was on him, her fists a blur of motion. He fell with a dull thud, his weapon clattering to the ground.

Elara stepped up to the massive doors, her fingers flying over the control panel. Her mind raced as she entered the codes she had memorised long ago, praying that SynapseCorp hadn't changed their security protocols. The screen flickered, and for a moment, nothing happened.

"Come on," Elara muttered under her breath, her heart pounding.

Behind her, Vex and Sera stood at the ready, their eyes scanning the hallway for any sign of approaching reinforcements. The sound of the approaching soldiers was growing louder, and they knew they were running out of time.

Finally, with a soft hiss, the doors to the neural hub slid open.

"We're in," Elara said, her voice filled with both relief and tension.

Vex nodded, his eyes hard. "Let's finish this."

Inside the command centre Rook watched the security feeds with cold, calculating eyes. The Unbound had made it into the neural hub, slipping past his guards and breaching the most secure part of SynapseCorp's tower. But Rook wasn't worried. He had been prepared for this.

"They think they've won," Rook muttered to himself, his lips curling into a cruel smile.

He stood, his movements slow and deliberate, as he activated the final override system. The neural network hummed to life around him, its tendrils reaching into every corner of the city. He could feel its power coursing through the system, controlling everything—every mind, every action.

"They've underestimated me," Rook whispered, his eyes gleaming with malice. "Let's show them what real control feels like."

Inside the neural hub the Unbound moved swiftly. The room was massive, its walls lined with rows of glowing terminals and pulsating wires that stretched like veins through the building. At the centre of the room stood the core of the neural network, a towering structure of steel and glass, its surface alive with energy.

"This is it," Elara said, her voice steady despite the tension. "Once we disable the hub, the entire network goes down."

Sera glanced at her. "How long will it take?"

Elara's fingers flew over the control terminal; her eyes focused on the data streams flashing across the screen. "A few minutes, but once we start, Rook will know we're here."

Vex stepped forward, his eyes locked on the core of the network. "Then we don't waste any time."

Elara took a deep breath and initiated the shutdown sequence. The screen blinked as the process began, the data streams slowing as the network started to unravel. But even as the system began to falter, a deep sense of unease settled over her.

Something wasn't right.

Suddenly, the room was filled with a low, ominous hum. The walls vibrated with energy, and the glowing lights of the neural core flared to life, pulsing with an eerie intensity.

"What's happening?" Sera demanded, her voice sharp.

Elara's eyes widened in horror as she stared at the screen. "He's activated the override."

Vex's jaw tightened. "What does that mean?"

"It means Rook still has control," Elara said, her voice filled with dread. "The hub is locking us out."

In the command centre Rook watched with satisfaction as the override system took hold. He could feel the network reasserting itself, tightening its grip on the city. The Unbound thought they could break free, but they didn't understand the full extent of his power.

"They're trapped," Rook whispered, his voice filled with venom. "And now, they'll see what real control feels like."

He activated the final phase of the override, sending a surge of neural energy through the system. The Unbound wouldn't just be defeated – they would be erased.

Inside the neural hub the room shook as the surge of energy tore through the network. Elara's heart raced as she fought to regain control of the system, her fingers moving frantically over the terminal. But the override was too strong. Rook had built a failsafe—something she hadn't accounted for.

"We're locked out," Elara said, her voice filled with frustration. "I can't shut it down."

Vex's fists clenched, his mind racing. They had come so far, but now, it felt like the walls were closing in around them. They couldn't afford to fail. Not now.

"There has to be another way," Vex said, his voice calm but firm.

Elara shook her head, her eyes filled with frustration. "The override is too powerful. Rook is still in control,"

Sera cursed under her breath. “Then we take him out. We take Rook down, and the system falls with him.”

Vex nodded. “We split up. Sera, you stay here with Elara and finish the shutdown. I’ll go after Rook.”

Sera’s jaw tightened, but she nodded. “We’ll get it done.”

Elara looked at Vex, her eyes filled with concern. “You can’t face him alone. He controls the network. He’s too powerful.”

Vex met her gaze, his voice steady. “We don’t have a choice.”

Without another word, Vex turned and sprinted out of the room, his heart pounding as he made his way toward the command centre. He knew Rook was waiting for him, knew the danger he was walking into. But he also knew that this was the only way.

The only way to end it all.

In the command centre, Rook stood alone, his eyes fixed on the door. He could feel Vex’s presence moving through the tower, feel the defiance radiating from him. But it wouldn’t matter. The network was too strong. Rook had built it to be unbreakable, and now, it would crush the Unbound once and for all.

The door slid open with a soft hiss, and Vex stepped inside, his body tense, his eyes locked on Rook.

“You’re too late,” Rook said, his voice calm and cold. “The override is in place. The network will survive, and you will fall.”

Vex’s jaw clenched, his fists tightening. “We’re taking you down.”

Rook smiled, a cruel, twisted smile. “You can try.”

CHAPTER 8: THE FINAL CONFRONTATION

The cold air inside the command centre was thick with tension as Vex and Rook stood facing each other, their eyes locked. The hum of the neural network pulsed through the walls, its power wrapping around the city like an invisible web. Vex could feel it—the control, the dominance, the weight of SynapseCorp's grip on every mind in Helios. But he could also feel something else: the growing rage inside him, the determination to break that control.

Rook's smile was cold and calculating as he took a step closer. "You've come all this way, thinking you could stop me," he said, his voice dripping with disdain. "But you've misunderstood. The network isn't something you can break. It's the future. It's progress."

Vex's fists clenched at his sides. "Your version of progress enslaves people. It takes away their freedom."

Rook's smile faded, replaced by a look of icy contempt. "Freedom is chaos. The network brings order. It makes people stronger, better. Without it, they are nothing."

Vex's eyes narrowed. "Without it, they're free."

Rook's expression darkened. "You think you're free? You've spent your life running, hiding in the shadows. That's not freedom. That's survival. The network is the only thing that can bring real power—real control."

Vex took a step forward, his body tense, his eyes locked on Rook. "Control isn't power. It's fear. And I'm not afraid of you."

For a moment, neither of them moved. The room was filled with the low hum of the network, the energy pulsing through the walls like a living thing. Vex could feel it pressing down on him, the weight of Rook's control. But he didn't waver. He had faced worse than this, and he wasn't about to back down now.

Rook's eyes gleamed with malice. "Then let's see what happens when you face the full force of the network."

With a flick of his wrist, Rook activated the neural override. The air in the room seemed to vibrate with energy as the network surged to life, its power reaching out towards Vex, trying to crush him, to bend him to its will.

But Vex wasn't like the others. He wasn't bound by the network's rules. He was Unbound.

As the energy surged toward him, Vex moved. His body flowed with precision and speed; his fists striking out in a blur of motion. Rook barely had time to react before Vex's fist connected with his chest, sending him staggering back.

Rook's eyes widened in shock. "How...?"

Vex didn't give him time to finish the question. He pressed forward, his strikes relentless, his movements fluid. The neural override couldn't touch him, couldn't control him. He was free.

Rook snarled, his expression twisting with fury as he fought back. His movements were enhanced by the network, guided by its precision, but Vex was faster. He dodged each strike, his body moving with an ease that came from years of training without the crutch of technology.

"You've spent your life controlling others," Vex said, his voice calm but filled with determination. "But you've never learned how to fight for yourself."

Rook's face contorted with rage. "You think you're better than me?"

"I know I am," Vex replied, his eyes cold.

With a final burst of speed, Vex drove his fist into Rook's chest, sending him crashing to the ground. The force of the blow knocked the wind out of Rook, and he lay there gasping for breath, his body trembling with shock and pain.

Vex stood over him, his breath steady, his eyes locked on Rook's defeated form. "It's over."

But even as he spoke, Vex could feel the network still pulsing through the walls, still active. Rook may have been defeated, but the system he had built was still alive, still controlling the city. And if they didn't shut it down, everything they had fought for would be lost.

Back in the neural hub Elara's hands moved frantically over the terminal, her mind racing as she fought to disable the override. The system was fighting back, layers of encryption blocking her every move. Sweat beaded on her forehead as the seconds ticked by, the pressure mounting.

"Come on," she muttered under her breath, her fingers trembling as she worked.

Sera stood beside her, her weapon at the ready, her eyes scanning the room for any sign of reinforcements. The sound of gunfire echoed in the distance, and Sera knew they didn't have much time.

"How long?" Sera demanded, her voice sharp.

"I'm almost there," Elara replied, her voice tight with frustration. "But Rook locked us out. I need a few more minutes."

"We don't have a few minutes," Sera growled.

Elara's heart raced as she pushed through the final layer of encryption. She could feel the system buckling under the strain, the data streams faltering as the shutdown sequence began. But it wasn't fast enough. Rook had designed the system to resist any external interference, and it was fighting back with everything it had.

Then, suddenly, the screen blinked green.

"I've got it!" Elara shouted, her voice filled with relief.

The neural hub's lights flickered, the hum of the network growing fainter as the system began to power down. The control that SynapseCorp had held over the city—the control that had kept the people of Helios bound to the network—was finally breaking.

In the command centre, Rook's eyes widened in horror as the lights around him flickered and dimmed. He could feel the network slipping away, its grip on the city weakening with every passing second. The control he had fought so hard to maintain was crumbling before his eyes.

"No," Rook whispered, his voice filled with disbelief. "This can't be happening."

Vex stood over him, his eyes cold. "It's over."

Rook's hands trembled as he reached for the control panel, his fingers desperate as he tried to reactivate the override. But it was too late. The network was failing, and there was nothing he could do to stop it.

"You've lost," Vex said quietly, his voice steady. "Helios is free."

Rook's eyes filled with rage as he stared up at Vex, his body trembling with fury. "You think you've won?" he spat, his voice shaking. "You think this is the end?"

Vex didn't answer. He didn't need to.

With a final, laboured breath, Rook's body slumped to the floor, his eyes still wide with shock. The man who had built SynapseCorp, who had controlled the minds of millions, was gone.

And with him, the network fell.

Outside the tower the streets of Helios were filled with chaos. The people, once bound by the neural network, were waking up—free from the control that had kept them in line for so long. Confusion reigned as the city's systems flickered and died, the once-perfect order of SynapseCorp's control unravelling before their eyes.

But in the midst of the chaos, there was a sense of hope. The people were free. The Unbound had won.

Back in the neural hub Elara leaned back in her chair, her heart still racing as the shutdown sequence completed. The network was down. The city was free.

Sera glanced at her, her expression still hard, but there was a glimmer of respect in her eyes. "You did it."

Elara nodded, her mind still reeling from the intensity of the battle. "We did it."

Vex entered the room, his face calm but filled with quiet determination. "It's over," he said, his voice steady. "Rook's gone. The network is down."

For a moment, the room was silent, the weight of their victory settling over them. They had fought for this—for freedom, for control over their own lives—and now, they had it.

But even as the relief washed over them, Vex knew that the fight wasn't truly over. The city was free, but the scars of SynapseCorp's control would take time to heal. The people of

Helios had been bound for so long, and it would take time for them to learn what it meant to be truly free.

But Vex wasn't afraid of that fight. He had spent his life fighting for freedom, and now he was ready to help the people of Helios build something new—something better.

"We've won the battle," Vex said quietly, his voice filled with resolve. "But the real fight is just beginning."

CHAPTER 9: AFTERMATH

The streets of Helios were eerily quiet in the aftermath of the network's collapse. Where once the city buzzed with the constant hum of neural control and automated precision, now there was only silence. The people, unshackled from SynapseCorp's grip, moved through the streets like ghosts, uncertain of what had just happened. For the first time in years, they were no longer bound by the network's constant surveillance, no longer controlled by Rook's invisible hand.

Vex, Sera, and Elara stood on the rooftop of SynapseCorp's central tower, looking out over the sprawling city below. The towers gleamed in the fading light of dusk, casting long shadows over the streets. But the city no longer felt like a machine. It felt alive, chaotic, and unpredictable.

Elara watched in silence, her mind still reeling from everything that had happened. The neural hub was down. The people of Helios were free. But freedom, she knew, was complicated.

"It feels strange," Elara said quietly, her voice barely audible over the wind. "All these years, we thought we were improving the city. Making it better. But now..."

Vex glanced at her, his expression unreadable. "You were doing what you thought was right."

Elara shook her head, her voice filled with doubt. "Was it? We took away their freedom. We controlled their every move."

Sera stepped forward, her eyes scanning the horizon. "We gave them back their freedom today. Now it's up to them to figure out what to do with it."

Vex remained silent, his mind already turning to the challenges that lay ahead. The collapse of the network was just the beginning. The people of Helios had been dependent on SynapseCorp for so long; they didn't know how to live without its guidance. And not everyone would welcome the change.

"There will be resistance," Vex said quietly. "Some people won't want to let go of the network. They'll fight to bring it back."

Sera's jaw tightened. "Then we'll deal with them. We didn't come this far to watch it all fall apart."

Elara's eyes darkened as she thought about what lay ahead. The battle against SynapseCorp had been brutal, but the fight to rebuild Helios would be even harder. The city had been shaped by control and order, and now it would be plunged into chaos.

"We can't just let the city fall apart," Elara said, her voice filled with determination. "We have to help them. We have to show them there's another way."

Vex nodded, his gaze fixed on the city below. "We will. But we can't force it. The people have to choose freedom for themselves."

The three of them stood in silence, watching as the sun set over the horizon. The future of Helios was uncertain, but for the first time in years, it was a future they could shape.

EPILOGUE: A NEW DAWN

The weeks that followed the collapse of SynapseCorp were filled with both hope and chaos. The city of Helios, once a beacon of technological control, was now free from the neural network that had bound it. But with that freedom came uncertainty.

Vex and the Unbound had become legends overnight. Stories of their fight against SynapseCorp spread like wildfire, and many people in the city looked to them for guidance. But Vex had always known that the real challenge would come after the battle was won. Freedom wasn't something that could be given—it had to be earned, understood, and embraced.

Elara worked tirelessly to help the city rebuild. She used her knowledge of SynapseCorp's systems to dismantle the remaining control mechanisms, freeing more people from the residual effects of the network. But as she worked, she saw the division growing. Some people missed the order and predictability the network had provided. They didn't know how to live without it.

"It's not going to be easy," Elara said one evening, as she and Vex stood on the outskirts of the city, watching the people below.

"No," Vex replied, his voice calm but resolute. "But it's worth it."

Elara nodded, though her heart was heavy with the weight of the responsibility they now carried. "Do you think they'll ever understand that freedom isn't just chaos?"

Vex smiled faintly. "They'll learn. It'll take time, but they'll learn."

In the months that followed, small factions began to form within the city. Some people wanted to restore parts of the network, craving the security and stability it had once provided. Others, inspired by the Unbound, embraced the chaos, eager to create a new society free from control. The city was divided, but it was also alive with debate, with possibilities.

Sera led efforts to help people adjust to their newfound freedom. She had always been a fighter, but now, her battle was different. She wasn't just fighting against an enemy—she was fighting for a future: one where people could live without fear, without control.

And Vex? Vex became a symbol of resistance, of hope. He didn't seek power or leadership, but the people looked to him, nonetheless. He had shown them what it meant to fight for freedom, and now he would help them find their way.

In the heart of Helios, the city was changing. The lights of SynapseCorp's tower, once a symbol of control, were dark. The streets, once monitored by drones and neural scans, were now alive with the sounds of people—free people, learning to live again.

The Unbound had won the battle, but the war for the soul of the city had only just begun.

And Vex, Elara, and Sera were ready for whatever came next.

www.ingramcontent.com/pod-product-compliance
Lightning Source LLC
LaVergne TN
LVHW091235150826
845673LV00003B/1151

* 9 7 9 8 8 9 6 1 0 7 5 6 9 *